For My Mother

Walter Lorraine (wl) Books

Say, Allen.
    [Once under the cherry blossom tree]
    Under the cherry blossom tree / Allen Say.
        p.   cm.
    Summary: A cherry tree growing from the top of the wicked
landlord's head is the beginning of his misfortunes and a better
life for the poor villagers.
    RNF ISBN 0-395-84546-7   PA ISBN 0-618-55615-X
    [1. Folklore—Japan.] I. Title.
PZ8.1.S27On   1997
398.2'0952
[E]—dc20   96-36278
                                            CIP
                                            AC

www.houghtonmifflinbooks.com

ISBN–13: 978-0-618-55615-1

Printed in the United States of America
WOZ 10 9 8 7 6 5

In joke houses (*yose*) throughout Japan, countless genera-
tions of audiences have been entertained by joke tales called
rakugo, which means dropped words or punch line. A per-
former, whose success is largely determined by his individ-
ual style of telling, always begins with a short tale—called
a pillow (*makura*)—intended to set the mood for the longer
stories to follow. *Under the Cherry Blossom Tree*, one of the
most popular and ancient *makura*, is a classic example of this
distinctive tradition of humor.

There once lived an old landlord in a small village in Japan. He lived in a big house all by himself. He owned all the land and every house in the valley.

He was so mean babies cried at the sight of him. He was so miserly he saved water by never taking a bath. He was so wicked he raised everyone's rent month after month until the villagers were very, very poor.

But even in a poor village spring is a beautiful time. There are eggs in every bird's nest, the air buzzes with honeybees, and the cherry trees bloom all at once.

"It's spring again. I can tell by those noisy birds. Chirp, chirp! Bah!" complained the old man.

One fine Sunday the villagers took whatever food and drink they had and went out to the meadow to picnic under the cherry blossoms. They ate and sang and danced the time away. It was the finest day of the year.

The miserly landlord went out to the meadow too. He took a basket of cherries and sat under a cherry tree all by himself. As he popped one cherry after another into his mouth he mumbled and grumbled and glared at his neighbors.

"Humm, look at them dance. That's all they ever do, dance and eat, eat and dance. They're just like children. Why are they so happy? Bah!"

Then, quite by accident, he swallowed a cherry pit. His face turned orange, blue, and purple. The cherry pit traveled around and around inside his body until it reached the top of his head, and there it stayed.

When the mean landlord awoke the next morning he felt something growing from the top of his head.

"Humm, what is this? A tree? One can't trust anything anymore. Now I won't be able to wear my hat. Bah!"

He was too stingy to see a doctor and too mean to be embarrassed. So he went around collecting rent with a cherry tree growing out of the top of his head.

The rainy season and the warm winds of early summer made the tree grow with amazing speed.

"Confound it! Nothing has grown on my head for thirty-seven years. And now this! The idiot tree must think my head is a garden. Bah!"

The tree grew and grew. And exactly a year later it burst into glorious bloom. The finest day of the year had come around once again.

The villagers were even poorer than before, but they had been saving all year for this day. They ate and sang and danced the time away and gathered around the landlord to marvel at his tree.

"What beautiful blossoms!"

"What does he use to make it grow?"

"Money, probably."

The miserly landlord was furious. "How dare you make fun of me! You won't get away with this! I'll raise your rent first thing tomorrow. See how you like *that*! Look at you, dancing and eating. That's all you ever do. Look at your children. They are fat! You're no better. And you are making fun of me! I'll fix you!"

The landlord grabbed the tree trunk with both hands, and with a swift pull uprooted the magnificent tree.

"He's gone mad!" the villagers shouted.

"He *is* mad!"

"Run for it, everybody!"

The villagers had never seen their landlord quite so angry. They quickly gathered their frightened children and ran home.

The next morning the landlord discovered a large hole in the top of his head.

"Humm…a hole, and it's empty. No wonder I felt light-headed last night."

He had never once seen a doctor, or a barber, or a tree trimmer, and he was not about to start now. So he went around collecting rent with a large hole in the top of his head.

The rains of summer soon filled the hole with water.

"Water in my head!" said the landlord. "Bah! Puddles are only good for children and mosquitoes! Now I'll have to sleep sitting up. And if I don't, there'll be puddles all over my bed. Troubles, troubles, troubles. Bah!"

But instead of mosquitoes, fish began to swim in the hole on top of the landlord's head. The fish got bigger and the landlord was rather pleased with that.

"Now I won't have to buy another carp from the fishmonger. I say it's money in the bank!" He came close to chuckling.

The landlord looked forward to his afternoon naps in his garden. He always sat up straight to be sure not to lose a single fish. And while he slept, the villagers enjoyed peaceful afternoons. That was the only time the wicked man was not complaining.

Tabo, the bravest boy in the village, was the first to notice the fish jumping on top of the landlord's head. One day after school, Tabo sneaked up to the landlord's house. The minute the old man began to snore Tabo signaled to his friends.

"Let's get some fish from the old miser," he whispered.

The boys got their fishing poles, and fished silently. They were careful not to get their hooks caught on the landlord's nose. Luckily for the boys, the landlord was a heavy sleeper. He snored and dreamed of rice cakes and delicious carp.

One day Tabo hooked the biggest fish the boys had ever seen. The great carp gave a mighty leap and jumped out of the landlord's head with a big splash. The landlord awoke with a start.

"Wha, what's this! Water! Cold water! Ugh! You brats! It's MY fish!"

With an angry shout he leaped to his feet. "You thieving brats! I am your landlord. How dare you take advantage of me and steal my fish!"

Yelling and screaming, the landlord chased the boys into the valley. He was so blind with rage he did not see a rock in front of him and he tripped.

"Auaah!" cried the landlord.

Then everything happened at once. The land-lord flew head-over-heels into the air. His feet sank into the hole in his head and suddenly his whole body disappeared! All that was left of the wicked landlord was a lovely pond in the valley.

When the children came out of hiding they saw carp swimming lazily in the deep clear water.

"Look at those magnificent fish," cried Tabo. The children ran home and spread the news.

When the villagers heard what had happened they were overjoyed. They gathered around the pond and sang and danced their time away. There were eggs in every bird's nest, the air buzzed with honeybees, and the cherry trees bloomed all at once.

And before long, the pond came to be known as the happiest spot in the valley.